BST Book Zero

Banana Split Timeline, Volume 0

Sol Quasar

Published by Pen Reilly, 2024.

This is a work of fiction. Similarities to real people, places, or events are entirely coincidental.

BST BOOK ZERO

First edition. October 30, 2024.

ISBN: 979-8224800247

Written by Sol Quasar.

Forward

The realm of superheroes is full of colorful characters and the amazing worlds that they inhibit. Some are fantastical! Some explore the darkness of humanity! Some stretch the imagination and go beyond what is possible! And some get retconned, but we don't talk about those. How superheroes interact with the world differs from story to story, dimension to dimension.

Banana Split Timeline began as a side project while I was working on Book 2 for Dragon's Blood. It was initially a casual thing, something I added onto whenever I felt like it. But I had become disheartened by the treatment of superheroes in fiction. In comic books, individual stories were drowned out by yearly events that "change everything". Character arcs had been reset and restructured so many times that nobody was recognizable anymore, not in a way that felt earned, and any stories that were accurate to the spirit of the characters would get all their progress erased or written over.

And in movies, the characters were watered down to be more palatable to corporations and general audiences—great for a night at the theater, but so very lacking in emotions and philosophy. I do not blame anyone for this; I know that everyone needs to feed their families somehow, and big blockbusters make the most money.

But there is a tragedy in the constant chase of the spotlight. It has caused a loss of identity in the characters that were supposed to mean something. It feels as if their true selves have eroded away, leaving behind empty shells. Now many are just money puppets who serve corporations or the military (intentional or not). If concepts had souls, then these souls were wiped clean, sanitized into nothingness.

One night in August 2021, I was possessed by a creative spirit, and an angry one at that. I awoke around midnight in a passion of righteous fury. I jotted down all of my frustrations and lay awake for a good hour or so afterward. I stared at the ceiling as I imagined all the ways I could fight against this madness [of modern superhero writing]. That is not to say that there are no more good superhero stories, but it feels so obvious that so many are chained down by executive control and obsession with The Next Big Thing.

I realized that there was a story to be told here- multiple ones in fact- and the only reliable way to tell them was to tell them myself. I originally began with only two Patrons, and thus, two timelines. At first, the themes were Space and Time, then they were Life and Death. Revival was created shortly after to round them out. The story of Life Timeline was what began this project and thus has the most artistic fire behind it. The story of Death Timeline allowed me to explain aspects hinted at in Life Timeline without detracting from the pacing in Life. The story of Revival Timeline then explains further aspects, namely Salavites, magic, and how those interact with the Patrons. The ultimate goal is that a person can read only one or two of the Timelines and still enjoy themselves, but those who read all three would be rewarded with an in-depth understanding of this universe.

For those who plan on reading all three, Life Timeline may seem like the "primary" timeline. However, it is equally valid to begin with Death or Revival Timelines. It is up to the reader to decide how they would like to enjoy the story. You could start with Revival, then read Death, then read Life. Do what you believe would be the most rewarding for you specifically.

I am not aware of any other books that explore three separate-yet-parallel stories in this way, at least not as timelines. If there is, then I applaud them and hope that this story is up to their standards. If not, then I suppose that I will have to be the first. Perhaps telling three intricate stories at once is too much to ask of myself- hell, they were originally planned to be novellas- but I am proud of what I have created and doing this has taught me much. I have lost nothing by creating this (except perhaps my sanity), and with this project, I hope to create my own unique stamp on the world. It is through passion that *Banana Split*

Timeline was born, and if that passion reaches anyone else, then I am content.

I chose spiders as the primary aesthetic because I feel that they are underappreciated in pop culture. They are framed as demons or monsters, feared instead of respected. Their precious round eyes and adorable faces are somehow seen as disgusting. Even Spider-Man does not want to be a spider. Sacrilege! A spider's unique appearance and fantastical skills are to be envied. Envied, I say! And I shall prove it.

Darcy's design as a spider was partially inspired by a spider I once saw at work. Someone had the bright idea of having me be the only sanitation worker for an entire shift on a busy day, yet nobody seemed to understand that I could only be in one place at a time. I was miserable. But during my work, I saw a white spider clinging for dear life against a mop bucket. Never before had I related to something so strongly. I still think about that white spider sometimes.

Warnings

Book 0 is rather short, but still involves spider creatures and a horror-style transformation sequence. Suicide is briefly considered by the main character, but quickly decided against. Even years after recovering from such a headspace, dangerous thoughts can still occur. If you find yourself struggling with these thoughts regularly, please consult a professional on the matter.

Book 0: Extra Note

The introduction was originally intended to each be included with each of the timelines (Life, Death, and Revival all starting with the same 1-2 chapters), but it was believed that this would be too confusing to readers, so I was required to separate these first two chapters into their own mini-book. Apologies for any confusion that may arise from this, my hands were tied. Simply read these first two chapters, then choose which timeline you wish to follow.

Chapter 1

The sky above Newstone City was a brilliant light blue hue and the sun dazzled like a diamond of fire. A pleasant, consistent breeze evened out the summer heat, creating that perfect sweet spot of temperature comfort. Civilians and superheroes alike stayed outside to enjoy the beautiful weather. One hero even sunbathed on a rooftop. Darcy saw him through the store window and sighed.

The store counter served as a barrier between Darcy and the rest of the world. They thought to themself,

What I wouldn't give to be anywhere else right now.

They tried reasoning to themself like they usually do.

At least I'm not stuck in fast food. Working the register at a tech store isn't the worst thing in the world. Still... not like I have any loyalty to this place. The only thing keeping me here is-

"Hello? I would like to make my purchase, please?"

"Sorry, ma'am." Darcy snapped back into focus. "Sorry, let me help with that."

Officially, customer service was meant to seem personalized, as if the employees were the customers' friends. But in complete honesty, it ran on scripts. The same smile and words were given to every customer. Every problem had steps to follow. Every person was recommended to get an account. Subscriptions were free for the first few months, then automatic payment started. Entering bank account information was a must. Getting a purchase was the focus. Words, words, words. To Darcy, it felt like being an NPC in a video game where everyone else was the main character.

Darcy had memorized everything they were supposed to do. They robotically plowed through every line of dialogue, day in and day out. The smile and the cheery attitude had been perfected to a T, an invisible mask to keep the customer base happy, and nobody suspected the wiser. In actuality, Darcy didn't feel anything at all. No joy from seeing a returning face, nor anger when someone ranted about an item not being returnable. They hardly paid attention to any of it; even doing change had been printed into muscle memory. Darcy's mind instead wandered off to other things.

I wonder how my mom is doing? I haven't called her in a hot minute, but it's not like I really have anything to report.

I wonder how Cleo and her family are? Probably better than me. Hell, she probably has her master's degree by now.

I wonder when Red will visit today? He was late last time. I hope he's taking care of himself.

An anthropomorphic insect approached them. He stood on two legs like a human would, but had four arms, an abdomen, and an exoskeleton. His two compound eyes had darkened pupils to allow him to focus on select objects. This species, the Venutians, originated from Venus, yet in a case of convergent evolution, their various races resembled different kinds of Earth insects. This particular one resembled a black harvester ant.

The Venutian approached the front desk.

"Ma'am, I have a problem."

"Yes, sir?"

"This charger won't go into my phone! See?"

"Sir, that isn't a charger, that's a headphone adapter, and it's meant for Alm-Tech phones. You have a Vance phone. It will need a Vance charger."

"Well, where are the chargers?!"

"Over there, sir." They pointed to an aisle only three feet away.

"Oh. They're... right there." He sheepishly scooted to the side. "Thanks."

"If you like, sir, we can transfer you to an Alm-Tech subscription. Our newest phones have a battery life so efficient that you will never need to charge it."

"Really? How does that work?"

"It's part of our Alm overhaul. Every device is getting a special model with an eternal battery. You will never want to buy from another company ever again."

"Huh. I might try it, then." He looked at the price tags. "Yikes! Or maybe not!"

Darcy chirped, "The cost is worth it!"

"Sure. Well, thanks anyway..." He looked at their name tag. "...Julia."

"Glad to help, sir."

A couple hours passed and a dull headache formed. The longer it lasted, the more it pounded. Darcy rubbed their fingers against their temples, which were hotter than usual.

God, please don't tell me I'm getting sick. Tomorrow's my only day off and I don't want to spend it in bed.

"I'm gonna go to the bathroom."

"Okay, I'll cover for you!" A young, perky coworker bounced to the register. Her name was Sarah... no, Sahara... no, maybe Sabrina... Darcy could never remember. Something starting with an S.

Despite using the bathroom and drinking some water, the feeling only became worse. Darcy's throat was now parched and a shaky feeling infested their muscles. Nonetheless, they returned to the front.

S's current customer- a tall man in his late forties- slammed his hands onto the counter.

"I demand a refund."

S flinched. "I'm sorry, sir. Can you tell me what went wrong?"

"I got a remote for my television and it doesn't work! Here it is." He set a busted remote down.

S held her hands together. "I-I'm sorry, sir, but your device is in no state for a return."

"Bullshit! I want my refund!"

S took a step back. "I'm sorry. I'll, um... do you have a receipt?

"Why the hell would I have a receipt? Just give me a new remote!"

Her voice cracked. "Oh-okay. I'll, um, I'll try-"

"No, I don't want *you*! It's obvious that *you* don't know what you're doing! Get me a manager!"

S looked down, now on the brink of tears. "I'm sorry, sir."

Darcy gritted their teeth. They stepped between the two.

"We cannot give a refund for a device in that state, sir."

"Are you a manager?"

"Yes," They lied. "And people with *your* attitude aren't welcome here."

He growled. "How dare you. The customer is always right! I deserve what I ask for!"

"And we would comply if you followed the procedure. But you have no receipt, no proof of purchase, not even any casing. You have *nothing*." They leaned forward. "Now **get out**. Before I call the authorities."

He stared them in the eyes, refusing to blink. "You wouldn't."

"Almond Industries has a superhero ambassador. If anyone causes trouble for the company, all we have to do is push a button to call him over. Do you want to deal with that? Or do you just want me to call the police and have you charged for harassment?"

The man stepped away. "You- you just lost a valuable customer today!"

"Trust me, you're not the kind of customer we value."

The customer finally left, slamming the door behind him. Darcy sighed with relief. They turned to check on S.

"Are you okay?"

S wiped away tears. "S-sorry. I didn't know what to do."

"You're okay. You didn't do anything wrong." They hissed, "Some people are just assholes. You don't deserve to be treated like that."

"Thank you. I'll-I'll try to stand my ground next time."

"How 'bout you go get some water? It'll help you restabilize."

"Okay. Thanks again."

Darcy gave her a nod.

After a couple more minutes, a superhero stepped into the store. He was a tall, spindly, awkward young man in a white-and-red costume with beige accents. He gave Darcy a cheery greeting.

"Hello!"

A smile shined across Darcy's face. "Hey, Red Arachnid. How're you doing today?"

"This year's Event ended, so heroes in the area have been helping with the cleanup. Usual stuff. How are *you* doing?"

Darcy rested their chin on their palm. "Oh, you missed it. A customer was trying to cause drama. One of those entitled people who think they're the center of the universe."

"Yikes. Need me to carry them out?"

"Nah, I was able to take care of it. Thanks, though." They gave a halfhearted chuckle. "I wish I could swear. 'Specially at the customers."

Red Arachnid gave a playful gasp. "But swearing is bad!"

"Heh. Some people deserve to be sworn at."

Red perused the aisles. He hummed as he admired the wares.

"It's all the same as yesterday," Darcy said. "And the day before that."

"I like looking."

This was another kind of script. Red Arachnid had come in every single day to browse the wares. He and Darcy would have a conversation about one thing or another, then he would be on his way. Sometimes he left without making a purchase at all. Darcy suspected that he only visited to see them, but pushed the thought away.

No, there's no way I mean that much to somebody. He probably just likes this location 'cuz it's so close to the Almond Industries headquarters.

Darcy coughed multiple times. Every time they did, the pressure in their head got worse. They said under their breath,

"God dammit."

Red leaned out of one of the aisles. "Are you okay?"

"Just a sore throat. And a headache. And maybe a fever."

"Julia, you work too hard! You need to take a day off once in a while."

"Red, if I don't work as much as I can, I won't be able to afford rent. Hell, I can barely afford food. Not everyone can be a sponsored superhero, you know."

He lowered his head. "Oh... I'm sorry."

"It's not your fault. I respect your hustle. I just need to keep working." They coughed and cleared their throat. "So how's your anxiety?"

He stepped back to the counter. "Well, I've been feeling a constant pain in my chest, but no panic attacks, so I'm happy."

"Wait, it's constant now? That doesn't sound good."

"It's just a bad day. I'm fine, don't worry."

"Have you thought about taking anxiety medicine? It could help."

"I don't know..." He fiddled with his fingers. "If I start taking medicine, I'll be dependent on it for the rest of my life."

"Well, yeah. There's no one-take cure for this stuff. 'Least I don't think there is. Taking medicine will help you function at the same level as people without anxiety. Think of it like wearing glasses."

"Oh, I actually heard that glasses were invented to make people's eyesight worse so they need to buy prescriptions."

Darcy rubbed their forehead. "That's not... I'm, like, eighty percent certain that's not true. Just think of it this way: anxiety medicine would help balance out your brain chemistry so you aren't so scared all the dang time."

He argued, "I'm not scared *all* the time."

"Dude. Last week, you started crying because you were at the front of the line and couldn't get your money out in time."

"I was just worried about holding everyone up! I didn't want them to hate me."

"Red, anyone who hates you for that reason is too petty to care about."

"Okay, you say that, but everyone's opinion is important." He paced back and forth as he spoke. "I need to think about what everyone is possibly thinking so I can compare and contrast what actions I should take that would result in the best-case scenario. And if I get anything wrong, I deserve to die. It's a perfect system!"

"Red... that's not normal."

"It's reasonable! It makes sense!"

"That's only 'cause you've gotten used to it."

"Well... still. I'm nervous about medications. I once had a single melatonin gummy and it knocked me out for eleven hours."

"Well, I can't force you to do anything you don't wanna do." Darcy sighed and rubbed their temples again. "Have you found anything yet?"

"I think so. I really like these wires."

"Oh yeah?"

"Yup." He placed it onto the counter. "I'm buying them because... I like them. I came to this place for no other reasons."

"I understand." Darcy did the transaction and made the change.

"Here you are."

Red Arachnid counted it. "Um... Julia? This isn't right."

"Huh?"

"The coins you gave me don't match up with the change."

"Oh! I'm sorry." Darcy took them back and recounted.

That was weird. I usually have this down-pat.

The building swayed, but Darcy ignored the sensation. They put together the change again and handed it back.

"Here you are. Sorry."

"It's okay! We all make... mistakes." His mask lenses squinted. "Wait, this isn't right, either."

"It-it isn't?"

"Way too many quarters here. I'm so sorry."

"No, I'm sorry! Let me try that again."

Panic built up inside them. They knew the change amount and how much Red needed back, yet no matter how hard they tried, they couldn't get their brain to connect the coins with the numbers they represented. The math didn't "click", and it had become apparent that they couldn't depend on muscle memory for this. They picked up a nickel with a sweaty hand.

Nickel. That's... that's five. Five cents. Or I could do a quarter, that's twenty five. What does twenty five do? A dime is ten. Pennies are ones. How many ones can I add to five to... to...

Darcy found themself on a chair in the break room. One of their managers stood in front of them with Red to the side. Darcy rubbed their head and sat up.

"Huh? What happened?"

The manager answered, "You passed out. We took you to the back to cool off."

"I... I passed out?"

"Don't worry, it's only been a few seconds."

"It was so scary," Said Red. "You just fell over!"

The manager asked, "How do you feel?"

Their headache had become even worse. The pain blocked out any thoughts. Their stomach rolled and churned like something was trying to escape.

"I think... I think I'm gonna throw up."

The manager sighed. "Then you should take the rest of the day off. I'll call in Jerry."

"Sorry-"

"It's fine. Go home." The manager answered robotically, the same kind of tone Darcy used when they were frustrated or disappointed in someone.

Red asked, "Um, do you have a way to get home, Julia?"

Darcy shook their head. "Usually take the tram."

They stood up, but soon lost their balance. The floor charged up at them. Red grabbed onto Darcy, saving them from collision.

"Woah!"

Darcy stuttered, "S-sorry. I-I don't think I can walk right now."

"Want me to carry you?"

"Are you sure? I wouldn't wanna waste your time."

"You're *not* a waste of time. C'mon."

Red let Darcy climb onto his back. He held them piggyback-style and exited the building.

Darcy drifted in and out of focus on the journey home. The gorgeous weather that they had envied just a few hours earlier now felt smothering.

The hot rays of the sun weighed on them like an electric blanket on maximum settings. Everything was so bright that Darcy had to close their eyes. But, admittedly, they couldn't tell if the temperature and brightness had actually changed or if it was just their fever. They rested their head against Red's shoulder.

"Thank you," They mumbled.

"No problem! I'm always up for helping a friend!"

"You... think of me as a friend?"

"Well, we've known each other for about four years now. There's a reason I go to your store every single day."

"It wasn't... the location?"

"I mean, that *does* help, but it's not the full reason."

He walked along in silence for a minute or two. He then said,

"Do you remember how we met?"

"Um... I was going to work. Or leaving work. Can't remember which. I was near the store. I saw you in the street. There was a crowd, I think, but nobody got close. You were panicking pretty hard."

"Yeah." He nodded. "I was still new to the company and my anxiety got bad. Everyone else just said empty comforts. 'You'll be alright.' 'There's nothing to be afraid of.' 'It's all in your head.' But you came right up to me. You knelt down so we'd be eye-level and you said, 'Tell me what's going on.' And I did. And you nodded along and acknowledged how *bad* I felt. It was... amazing."

"I... didn't think my actions affected you that much."

"Don't tell this to anyone else, but..." He sighed. "Everyone tries to change what I'm feeling. Even Mister Harrell. I know that making everyone happy is important, but you're the only person I know where I don't have to... wear a fake face. Even your advice is for my sake; I'm just too scared to try it."

"I can't really blame you, to be honest. I struggle with taking care of myself, too. I mean, hell, I refused to take it easy and then collapsed at work. Come to think of it, telling you what to do kinda makes me a hypocrite."

"But are you wrong?" He gave an accepting sigh. "There's... something wrong with me. Something is wrong with my brain. I *know* there is. But I've had anxiety for as long as I can remember. It's practically part of my identity. So if I treated my anxiety, would I still be the same person? Would I lose the part of myself that makes me patient, empathetic, or compassionate? Would I even know how to function without it?"

"Maybe you're all those things not because of the anxiety, but in spite of it."

"I don't know... after all, how do we determine which parts of ourselves are inherent? Which behaviors are developed because of our circumstances and which parts are forged into our souls?"

"Maybe it's up to the choices we make?"

"But our choices are informed by our pasts, where and how we're born, and we don't choose that. So really, do we have free will at all? Maybe our fates were always meant to be determined by other people. Maybe fate is a single train track destined for hell."

"Man... I think my headache is getting worse."

"I'm sorry. My thoughts get bad when I let them run like this. I shouldn't allow that."

"You're good. I'm just not in the best state for philosophy right now. But... thank you. For considering me your friend."

"Yeah! Thank you for being my friend, too. Even if I can be a burden."

"You're not a burden."

Red didn't reply. After a few minutes of awkward silence, he asked,

"So, how are you holding up?"

"Eh."

"I guess I should hurry up the pace, then."

"You're okay. We're not far now."

"Alright." A pause. "So, uh... do you like working for Almond Industries?"

"It's alright. Feel like I can't complain."

"Yeah..." More silence. "Are you... happy?"

They sighed. "I dunno. Part of me wants out of this stupid job, but another part of me is just grateful I have a job at all. But I don't want to waste my life as a cog in a corporate machine. I wanna *learn* stuff. I wanna see new things! I want out of the... the monotony."

Red nodded along. "I envy your drive. I don't know where I'd be without my sponsorship. Being a company ambassador has given me a purpose. I was hardly a superhero before this."

"Hard to imagine you as a civilian."

He laughed. "I can't, either!"

They stopped at Darcy's home. The apartment building had been built out of gray bricks, rickety windows, and air conditioning units that hung halfway out of the building. Red set Darcy down.

"Need help getting inside?"

"Think so, yeah. I feel like I might collapse again."

He helped them across the ragged carpeting, up the squeaky stairs, and to their door. Their apartment itself only consisted of three compact rooms: a kitchen, a bedroom, and a bathroom. Darcy had to walk through the kitchen to get to the bedroom. It only had a twin-sized bed and a small drawer, but that was enough for them. After all, if they weren't working, they were sleeping. Darcy crashed onto the bed.

"*God.*"

Red rubbed the back of his neck. "It's funny, but this is bigger than my room at the headquarters."

"Really?"

"Mister Harrell loves his minimalism. But I don't have to pay for rent, so it balances out."

He pressed a button on the side of his mask. The lenses deactivated, losing their pale green glow.

Darcy sat up. "Why'd you turn off your mask?"

"Because I wanted to talk to you in private. Um... are you comfortable with me in your bedroom?"

"I literally don't have the energy to care. What'd'ya wanna say?"

"Well... what if I told you that there's an employer who you might enjoy working with? The pay is good and you can set your own hours. They never exceed your boundaries and the perks are *super* cool."

"Heh. Sounds too good to be true."

"Maybe in America. But there are things in this world that are better than the bare minimum, and I think this job could make you really happy."

Darcy shrugged. "Alright, then. What's the job?"

"It's helping people. Kinda like a superhero! You can even use it to become a superhero if you want. Or you could stay low to the ground. It's all valid. You could stop crime, deliver supplies, fight monsters... anything you're comfortable with."

"Helping people, huh? What the hell, I'll try it. How do I sign up?"

"I'll have to talk to someone first and see if they're interested. If they are, they'll set up a meeting with you. It might take a few hours, though."

"'Kay." They gave a thumbs-up. "See ya."

"Bye!" He turned his mask back on and gave them a wave. "I hope you recover well!"

"Thanks. And hey!"

He stopped at the bedroom door. "What?"

"Don't forget to take care of yourself, 'kay? Drink your water. Eat some food."

Even though Red's mask covered his entire face, his tone betrayed his smile.

"Aren't **I** supposed to be taking care of **you** right now?"

"Just don't want you to forget."

"I'll try. You drink some water, too. See you in a couple days, hope everything goes well." He shut the door behind him.

Darcy forced themselves into pajamas and sat by the bedroom window. The window connected to a fire escape that led to the roof above and alleyway below. Lacking the energy to move again, Darcy rested their head against the window and shut their eyes.

— — —

Evening had crept in at some point. It bathed Darcy's bedroom in a brilliant orange hue. Darcy would admire the beauty if they didn't feel even worse than before. Their limbs were sore, their headache pounded like a hammer, and their throat felt sharp and hot.

Water.

They lumbered into the bathroom and drank from the sink. As thirsty as they were, though, all the water did was make their throat feel muddy and fill them with nausea.

Ugh. Why?

Back in the bedroom, they pulled back the covers and readied to fall in. Something stopped them, though—a small dark speck in the corner of their eye. It sat on their pillow and moved slightly.

Huh? Darcy leaned closer to look. A house spider. Darcy watched it in a mixture of confusion and pity.

"What are you doing here, little guy? There isn't food here."

The spider didn't answer, of course. It simply cleaned its little fangs with its pedipalps. Darcy sighed.

"Here. Let's move you." It hurt to talk- like rubbing together burning sticks inside their throat- yet something about it was comforting. Darcy removed the name tag from their uniform and set it next to the spider. It crawled onto the name tag. Darcy slowly moved it to a room corner and let the spider off. It settled into the shadows, content.

"Goodnight, bud."
With that, Darcy, too, settled down to sleep.

Chapter 2

Revival Patron

Or, at least, Darcy *tried* to sleep. Their body wrestled with itself in both exhaustion and discomfort. Their head begged for rest, yet refused to lose consciousness. Their stomach felt as if it were constantly turning. Their comforter felt both too hot and too thin, soon drenched in sweat. Darcy tossed and turned in their aches and nausea.

"Why?" They mumbled to no one. "Why..."

Someone knocked on the door. Red Arachnid's voice came from the other side.

"Julia, are you still awake? I'm sorry to come back, but I just got so worried. I kept thinking about you... I just... can I come in?"

Speaking still hurt, but Darcy still answered him.

"Yeah. Come in."

Red entered the room with an ice pack in hand. "Again, sorry about being that person who visits you in the middle of the night, but my anxiety convinced me that you were in trouble and I got an ice pack and your door was unlocked and-"

"Ice pack. Head."

"Right, yeah."

He knelt down next to Darcy's bed and placed the ice pack against their forehead.

"How does that feel?"

"Good. Thank you."

Darcy flinched as pain shot through their stomach. They curled up with their arms around their torso.

"It hurts..."

"Want me to get some water?"

"Please."

Darcy must have passed out again, because the next time they came to, they heard voices next to their bed. Darcy couldn't see the speakers without turning around, so they simply stayed in place, kept their eyes closed, and listened.

Red's voice: "I'm really scared. What if she doesn't wake up?"

A young, ethereal voice: "Her heart is still beating. There's still hope."

"But..." A sob. "I'm sorry, I just... she's my only friend. If I lost her, I don't know what I'd do."

"It'll be okay. I mean, not her dying, but the situation being... you get what I mean. Things can still turn around."

The two stepped over to the other side of the bed, the side that Darcy was facing. The ethereal voice said,

"I have something that can help, but I want her consent before I try using it. Can you wake her up?"

"I'll try."

Red placed a hand on Darcy's shoulder. He gently moved them back and forth.

"Julia?"

Darcy opened their eyes. Although they had guessed that the ethereal voice wasn't human, their appearance still surprised them: a silhouette that stood at about seven and a half feet tall, with its only visible features being eight blue eyes that glowed in the dark.

Darcy held back a scream. They didn't want to frighten whoever wanted to help them, and it would be painful to scream right now anyway. So, they simply asked,

"Who?"

Red Arachnid said, "Julia, this is Revi. They're related to someone I work for."

"Hello," Said Revi. "Um, do you remember helping a spider earlier tonight?"

"Uh... yeah."

"Well, that was a secret test. And you passed! So that makes you eligible for a job. But when I got here to give you the offer, you were sick. You *are* sick."

"Thanks," Darcy replied dryly. "I didn't notice."

"Um, if it's alright, can I look into your personal future? It requires physical contact, but it'll let me see the most likely things that could happen to you."

"Sure."

Revi moved closer, their footsteps surprisingly light. A chitinous hand with three claws rested upon Darcy's skull.

Darcy saw themself resting all day the next day. They didn't have the energy to even get out of bed. Red Arachnid stayed by their side, helping them eat and drink. The day after that, Darcy had enough strength to return to work, but kept having to stop so they could sit down and rest. Darcy saw brief conversations, but the moments never lasted long enough for them to know what was being said. After a few days of no change and no recovery, one of the managers approached Darcy with a pink slip. Darcy returned home and crawled into bed as their surroundings became bleak.

Darcy sat up. "They fire me?!"

Revi pulled their hand back. "Oh, man. That doesn't look good."

"They *fire* me?! I worked my butt off for nearly eight years and they-!"

Darcy's throat burned, forcing them to stop. They coughed and Red handed them a cup of water. Darcy graciously drank as much as they could. It still made their throat feel like mud, but it was better than before.

Revi said, "I'm really worried about that bleakness at the end. I think that symbolized your health."

Red asked, "Wait, so you think Julia is going to...? Is she gonna die?"

"Not if I can help it." Revi said to Darcy, "I can save you. I can make it so you'll heal from this *and* you won't get sick from any other human diseases. You'll be safe."

"What's the catch?"

Revi looked down. "Well... when my siblings and I heal people, it also transforms them. Makes them look like us."

Darcy squinted at Revi. Even with their eyes adjusted to the darkness, it was difficult to tell what Revi was. Darcy had their suspicions, but wanted to be certain.

"Turn on the light."

"I can do that," Said Red.

As Red turned on the bedroom light, Darcy prepared themself for anything. At worst, an eldritch demon. At best, a fluffy bunny with some extra eyes. In reality, Revi was neither of the two.

With the light on, it became obvious that Revi was some sort of arthropod. They stood on their hind legs like a Venutian, but the plates of their exoskeleton were sorted differently. The exoskeleton was deep black everywhere except for the jaw, torso, and claws, which were blue. At the center of the forehead rested a blue symbol in the shape of a diamond. Pale yellow fluff covered their neck, wrists, and ankles. The fluff appeared to be soft and thick, like chinchilla fur—Darcy had to restrain themself from reaching out and touching it. Revi's jagged mouth opened and closed when they spoke, revealing hollow insides.

"This is me."

"Wow..."

Darcy had heard of demons. Sometimes, a rumor would spread about strange creatures appearing or monsters lurking in the shadows. Personally, Darcy had never paid heed to them; after all, in a world of aliens and superheroes, what point was there to freaking out about demons?

But then again, there were some things that a person couldn't prepare themselves for. Darcy tried not to appear unnerved, but they couldn't stop staring at Revi's eyes. Only the two large, primary eyes had eyelids. These black eyelids were only semi-transparent; Revi's blue eyes and lighter-blue pupils could still be seen underneath them even when fully closed.

"Uh... are you alright?" Revi asked. "Am I too scary?"

"No, no. Just didn't expect an arthropod to have eyelids. Venutians don't have those."

"Oh, yeah! They help with facial expressions."

"Hm. So if I let you help me, would I look exactly like you?"

"Not exactly. You would become an arachnomorph. Here, let me show you a diagram."

Revi clapped and a cloud of blue sparkles appeared. The sparkles became a clipboard with a single sheet of paper on it. On the paper was a child's drawing of Revi standing next to a small white spider with blue limbs and claws. While Revi only had two arms, the spider had six, as well as chelicerae on the cheeks and an abdomen behind them.

Revi said, "My art isn't very good, but the white spider is what you would look like. Well, the default. The white is a nice, blank color while the blue is, um... well, it's just my favorite color."

"That's valid. So... would I... get powers?"

"Mm-hm! Super strength, super agility, sticking powers, making your own silk... and the more in-tune you become with your spider instincts, the easier it will be to use these powers."

"Wow."

"But the transformation is permanent. We won't be able to change you back. Even if you don't work with us, you'll still be an arachnomorph. For the rest of your life..."

Darcy considered rejecting Revi's help. If the vision was accurate and Darcy's health would only decline, then maybe...

Maybe I wouldn't need to worry about being alive anymore.

This wasn't a new thought. If Darcy was... gone... they wouldn't have to worry about anything. Not getting fired, not paying rent, not finding food... they'd have no concerns at all.

But then their mother wouldn't have any family left. They wouldn't get to see Red Arachnid anymore. Darcy wouldn't be able to spend time with either of them. They wouldn't get to try all the foods they've been curious about. They wouldn't ever lie down in the grass again or explore a forest. They wouldn't be able to learn anything new about the world. They would never know what is just around the corner of time.

"...Let's do it."

Revi nodded. "Any particular design you want to give this form?"

"Uh... I'm... not artistic..."

Red piped up, "If you want, I could- never mind."

"What is it?"

Red rubbed his arm and looked away. "It's nothing. Forget I said anything."

Revi broke the awkwardness by saying, "Well, if you ever want to change the colors or add cool patterns, you can do that when you molt."

"I'll molt?"

"Uh-huh! Arachnomorphs molt once a year, in spring. You'll become a whole half-inch taller!"

Darcy didn't bother hiding their sarcasm. "Wow. That's crazy."

"I know, right? In twenty-four years, you'll be an entire foot taller!"

Darcy was only five-foot-two. While they weren't sensitive about their height, they *did* envy the bodybuilders on television and magazines.

"Would I become big and strong?"

"Not with the current design, sorry." Revi quickly added, "But you can still customize the colors!"

"That's fine. I'll just go with the default colors."

"Okay. Do you want the transformation to take place over a few hours, or for everything to change all at once? Faster would be more stressful on your body, and with your illness, it might even be painful. But it'll be, y'know, faster."

"I'll go with that, then."

"Are you sure?" Asked Red.

"I wouldn't say it if I wasn't sure."

"Sorry. I just... I don't wanna see you in pain."

"I'm already in pain. And if this'll make it so I don't get sick anymore, then I wanna get this over with as quickly as possible."

Revi gave a slow nod. They made their clipboard disappear in a cloud of blue sparkles.

"How would you like to ingest the transformation? Food? Water?"

"Do your favorite drink."

"Apple juice?"

"Sure."

Revi conjured a glass full of apple juice and handed it to Darcy. Darcy took a sip. Its cool, smooth texture had a sweet tint to it that helped it go down easily.

"Oh, *wow*. Red, you want some of this? It's actually really good."

"Um, no thanks. I'd like to stay human."

"Fair enough."

Darcy quickly finished the rest, then laid back down. They could already feel their insides shifting.

"I think it's starting..."

Revi tapped their claws together. "Okay, um, I'm really sorry, but I'm sensing a call from one of my employees. I'm gonna have to leave for a bit, but I'll be back as soon as I can."

"That's okay."

"Good luck!"

Revi vanished into thin air. Darcy then looked to Red.

"It's okay if you wanna go."

"I can't."

"It'll probably be stressful."

"I can't just leave you. If it's okay... I want to stay."

This filled Darcy with relief. Although they put on a brave face, they were grateful to not have to go through this alone.

"Thank you."

Red stayed next to Darcy's bed as the transformation started. It began with Darcy's fever peaking, followed by an acute pain in their stomach. The pain spread outward; it felt as if Darcy's entire skeleton were trying to escape. Their breathing became short and labored. They sat up with a scream. Red rubbed their back.

"Is there anything I can do?" He asked.

"I... I don't know... Rrrrr**rrgggg**."

Their body violently shivered. One of their hands tightened around their ribs while the other held Red's hand. Their fingers exploded into claws, tearing open the skin on their hands. The skin on the rest of their body ripped open as well, as if something was trying to escape. Darcy squeezed their eyes shut and tightened their grip on Red's hand.

"It hurts..."

Red whimpered from the pressure, but said, "I'm here. It's gonna be okay. I'm here."

More claws tore through the sides of Darcy's pajamas. Chelicerae burst out of their cheeks and more of their skin peeled off. It felt like someone removing a giant bandaid. Darcy coughed and leaned forward. They lost the contents of their stomach onto the bed. Their throat burned and their eyes stung. They could barely breathe.

Darcy didn't know if it was the strain of the transformation or simple exhaustion, but their consciousness went dark. The last thing they remembered was Red's voice calling out to them.

Death Patron

By the time Darcy awoke, dawn had brought a ruby-red glow to the bedroom. Darcy lay in someone's arms, held in a close cradle. They saw a human face with olive-green eyes and auburn-red hair. His gaunt cheeks were wet with tears. But upon realizing that Darcy had awakened, hope sparked in his eyes.

"You're... you're okay."

Darcy made a tiny smile. "Hi. I'm alive."

"Welcome back. How do you feel?"

"I feel... tired. Hungry. But not sick."

No pain remained from the transformation, not even a single ache, but by god did Darcy feel lethargic. They didn't even want to move their head to look around. But their stomach felt so empty that they would eat a boot if presented with one. Darcy wriggled in Red's arms.

"Food."

"Here. Let me help you up."

Darcy wobbled to their feet. Just like Revi's drawing, Darcy now had blue chitinous shins ending in three blue claws. Their thighs were white and fuzzy, like the bristles of a toothbrush. The legs connected to a plain-gray torso. Darcy put a hand against their belly as it growled.

"Stomach's still in the same place."

"Um, yeah, I guess so."

Red helped Darcy walk across the bedroom. The switch from five digits on each foot to only three was quite a change for them. Each foot had two claws in the front and one in the back, attached to the heel. This changed the distribution of weight and made Darcy stumble a bit, but Red caught them every time. As they moved along, Darcy glanced at the corner of the room. Their comforter had been wadded up into a ball and appeared damp in some spots. An acrid smell wafted from it.

In the kitchen, Darcy sat at the table while Red checked the fridge. He pursed his lips and looked back to them.

"Um... bad news: you don't have anything. Unless you count an empty milk carton."

"Aw, man. I forgot..."

Darcy rubbed their face with their claws and realized that the top half of their face was covered in fuzz as well. They then sighed and leaned an elbow against the table. Their hunger made them feel hollow inside.

"Oh man.... Well, there's garbage in the alleyway outside..."

Red frowned. "We're not doing that. I'll buy you something to eat. Stay here."

"Get meat. Lots of it."

Red put his mask back on and left.

Darcy repeatedly tapped their claw against the tabletop. They fantasized about their first meal as a spider.

A well-done beef burger with thyme seasoning. Or an oven-baked slab of ham drenched in honey. Maybe a pulled-pork sandwich and barbecue sauce...

Their stomach growled again. Darcy smacked their forehead against the tabletop.

Dammit, stop thinking about food! You'll only make it worse!

A distraction was in order. Darcy journeyed to the bathroom to wash themself up.

The bathroom was only a few feet large and square-shaped. The shower had the same water pressure as California's precipitation did this summer—light, faint, and rarely satisfying. Still, it was enough for Darcy to wash themself clean of anything left behind from the transformation.

Similar to the legs, the arms began with white fuzz and ended in blue chitin and three blue claws. A black, soft substance covered Darcy's joints. Strangely enough, the extra arms moved with just as much ease as the original ones did, like Darcy instinctively knew what to do with them. The same couldn't be said for their abdomen, however. It lay behind them like a stiff tail, being a similar size to their head. It had two holes at the end, one a little lower than the other.

I'm a spider now, so I guess this is how I would make silk. That could be cool to figure out.

Next was drying off— Darcy checked their face in the mirror as they did so. Their round head now had eight eyes to it: two primary ones and six secondary ones flanking them. Although Darcy knew that spiders had multiple eyes, they were still surprised; after all, their vision was still the same.

In school, science class taught that the brain takes information from the eyes and makes it all make sense. Maybe my brain is translating my new eyesight into something I can understand?

The eyes themselves were still the same dark brown hue that Darcy had as a human. Darcy actually found themself a bit disappointed by this; they had hoped to get something a bit more dramatic, like cherry-red or dandelion-yellow.

Maybe I can try for a different eye color when I molt next spring. If I remember by then.

Darcy placed a claw against their chelicerae. It was the same blue chitin as their forearms and shins, and like those parts, it had a certain shine to it. They opened their jagged mouth and found sharp, triangular teeth. This made Darcy smile.

I can feel like a shark now!

Their jaw was like their joints in that it was soft, black, and flexible. Darcy then looked down to their neck, which was protected by a ruffle of some sort. Many blue bristles pointed outward from their neck. Darcy ran a hand through the neck-bristles; it was like touching pine needles.

"Guess I have some protection..."

Their voice sounded different now, too. Even Darcy's mother wouldn't recognize it.

I... don't have to be Julia anymore...

They no longer had Julia's hair. They no longer had Julia's skin. They no longer had to carry her name. And, sure, their eye color was still the same, but at the end of the day, brown was really common.

Darcy gingerly put a hand against their cheek. Their claws brushed against white fuzz, then trailed down their face. The claws clicked against their left chelicerae before stopping at their jaw. Darcy's free hands clung to the sink; their grip tightened as their shoulders shook. Darcy's entire body trembled as tears dropped into the sink.

I have my own face.

"Are you okay?"

Darcy turned and found Red Arachnid in the bathroom doorway with his mask back on, but still inactive. They wiped away the tears and gave him a genuine smile.

"Yeah. I feel amazing."

Red had bought a couple meatball subs, which Darcy soon devoured. He sat next to them in the kitchen as they ate.

Darcy tried to eat the food slowly- they honestly tried- but hunger overpowered restraint. They ripped through the meal; their chelicerae protracted fangs, which tore off chunks of the bread and carried them to Darcy's mouth. Their teeth cut through the meatballs like butcher knives. Sauce painted Darcy's mouth and chin, but they didn't care. All that mattered was getting the food into their stomach as quickly as possible. They didn't even taste it.

Red watched Darcy with the utmost fascination. Darcy only noticed his stare after they finished the first sub. They looked at him, then at the table. They wiped both it and themself down with a handful of napkins.

"Sorry. Am I grossing you out?"

"No, no! Um, well..." He rubbed the back of his neck. "I've been meaning to ask... are you okay with this form?"

"Out of the two bodies I've had in my life, it's quickly becoming my favorite."

"Really? That's good at least."

Darcy began the second sub, slowly this time. They enjoyed how their teeth cut through the meatballs and the flavor that the sauce gave to the bread. After they finished it, they leaned back in their chair with a sigh.

"Wow. You saved me."

"I'm glad you liked them. I like my meatball subs with the meatballs first. I would pour them into a little bowl and eat them with a fork. Then, I would eat the bread. That was my favorite part! Because then the sauce would make it all nice and soggy." He rubbed his arm. "Gosh, that sounds weird to say out loud."

"Hey, you're valid. We all have different ways of eating things. When I was a kid, I once saw someone make toast by putting bread into a microwave instead of a toaster."

"Oh my."

Darcy glanced at Red's empty side of the table. "So what are you having?"

"Oh, um... I ate on the way back. Don't worry about me."

Darcy was uncertain, but decided not to push it.

"Thank you for being here with me," They said. "I appreciate it so much. I feel like I can't even put it into words."

"I'm glad I could help. It's nice to know I mean so much to someone."

"Are you kidding? You mean the world to- uh, the world." Darcy quickly added, "You're a superhero, so you mean a lot to everyone."

"I guess so, but being a figurehead is different from being a friend. And I just..." He took off his mask again. "I'm glad I could pay you back for being so kind to me."

But I've just been doing basic kindness. Is... is his home life so bad that my behavior feels like something special? Guess I can't blame him—I've been in a similar situation. If he and I never met, then I would be...

Darcy pushed away the thought with a smile. "I guess this officially makes us friends?"

Red beamed. "Really? Um, I mean, if that's okay with you."

"Yeah. And I think I'm ready to share my true name with you."

He tilted his head to the side. "I don't understand."

"I was born with the name Julia, but over the years, I found that my identity was, uh... different from that."

Darcy then realized how ill-prepared they were for this conversation. They had only come out once, and that was to their family. It was easy then—Darcy's parents had assured them beforehand that they supported their child's identity, and afterwards, they had celebrated the event with a banana split. It was magical.

But how would Red react? Even nice people can misunderstand something like this. What if... he refuses to understand? I don't think I can lose a friend again...

"What is it?" Red asked.

Whatever! Just tear off the bandaid!

Darcy took a deep breath and sat up. They explained as quickly as possible,

"I don't have a gender. I used to be female, but I removed that from my identity. Same with my birth name. So I'm agender and that's that. My true name is Darcy."

Red seemed to need a moment as the cogs turned in his head. He watched Darcy's expression, then gently took one of Darcy's hands with his own.

"Darcy..."

He shook their hand with vigor. "Wow, Darcy! What a pretty name! It's so nice to finally officially meet you! Hi! My name's Red- wait, no that's my hero name." He laughed nervously. "Sorry."

Darcy laughed along in relief. "No problem."

"My name is Oliver Vermilio. I'm onegender. Allogender? I, um... sorry. What I mean to say is that I'm male. So, uh... do you use 'they' and 'them'?"

"Yeah, that's right. Do you go by 'he/him'?"

"I think so! I haven't found anything else that I vibe with. But wow! This is so cool! It feels like we finally know each other!"

Darcy's face relaxed. "Yeah." A moment passed. "So... do we hug now, or...?"

"Yes! I love hugs!"

Oliver was a bit skinny- to a concerning level, actually- yet still gave a warm hug. Darcy wrapped all their arms around him and rested their head against his chest.

Oliver said, "Do you think I'm the first person to get a six-armed hug?"

"Maybe? Sorry, I can do just two if it's uncomfortable..."

"No no, you're okay! It feels nice."

After the duo separated from the hug, Revi reappeared. They immediately smiled upon seeing Darcy.

"Oh, thank Time, it worked!"

"It did," Darcy replied. "Thank you."

"And you're adjusting well?"

"I think so. Feels pretty good, all things considered."

"That's such great news! I'm so glad! Okay, so now that you're good and present, I can officially ask you about something."

"What is it?"

"Well, remember how I told you about the spider being a secret test?"

Darcy snapped their claws together. "Oh, yeah! And then you said something about a job?"

"Yup! You see, there's me and my two older siblings. We're called Patrons!"

"Wait," Said Oliver. "Revi, are you sure you should be using the exact terminology? Shouldn't you be, um... vague?"

Revi shrugged. "Not really a point in keeping a secret since the person in question is an arachnomorph now."

"That's, um... fair."

Revi clapped. "Okay! So each Patron represents an aspect of existence! The eldest sibling Life, the middle child Death, and the 'baby of the family', Revival. That's... me. Sadly."

Darcy said, "Hey, if it helps, you don't look like a baby to me."

"I'm actually only three feet tall. I only make myself look older so people will take me seriously."

"Oh."

Revi sighed. "Yeah..." Perking up, they said, "So! People who work for Patrons are called warlocks! Warlocks get a bunch of cool perks, like superpowers, food, money, and I even provide homes for-"

"Wait, back up. Did you say 'food' and 'money'? As in... that stuff is provided by the company?"

"Well, we're not really a company. We're just kinda... Patrons. And of course we provide that stuff! What kind of a person wouldn't want to keep their employees alive?"

"Clearly, you've never worked in America."

"Ha-ha! That's true! But anyways, a food box is given to every warlock. You only get one, though, so if you lose it, that's on you."

"What's a food box?"

"I'll show you!"

Revi conjured a blue box with a whiteboard and marker attached to it. They wrote "6-inch sausage pizza" onto the whiteboard. They opened the box and pulled out a sausage pizza with a diameter of six inches.

"Tada!"

"Woah!" Darcy touched it. "It isn't even greasy! And it's still hot, too. How did you do this?"

"The box has a teeny tiny piece of my power."

Oliver added, "It can only make food, though. You'd have to get the plates and silverware by yourself."

"Wow..." *If I had this, I wouldn't have to worry about affording food anymore. The money could be put towards rent and clothes. I could finally get some new clothes!*

"How much is the pay?"

"It's like a commission thing. Every time you help us, you can choose a reward: money or a new power!"

"A new power?"

Oliver explained, "All the Patrons are spider-themed. When someone is hired as a warlock, they are given a bit of a Patron's power, so they get spider-themed abilities. With every successful job, they can unlock even more abilities, like wrist barbs and venom glands."

"Huh. I see. So after I do a warlock job, I can either choose to be paid money or paid with a new power. Did I get that right?"

Revi nodded. "Yup! And you get the food box no matter what."

"Okay. So what kind of jobs are there?"

"Well, it changes based on the Patron. Death knows more about it than I do. If you want, I can call them over for you?"

"Yeah, sounds good."

"Awesome! They'll be here in a sec!"

After Revi disappeared, Darcy asked Oliver,

"So, you work for a Patron."

Oliver looked down and played with his fingers. "Yeah. Sorry I couldn't tell you before. It's supposed to be top-secret. Not even Mister Harrell knows. The Patrons are worried that if everyone knew about them, they'd be attacked and drained of their power."

"What would happen then?"

"Well, let's take Death Patron for example. They can detect a person's death and help souls move on to the afterlife. Imagine if that power was in the hands of a corporation."

Darcy grimaced. They pictured subscriptions and fees, loans and debts. People not being allowed to move on until they or a loved one paid enough money, or because they weren't a VIP. And what would happen to the lower class, the homeless, and the people in prisons?

Darcy shook their head. "Yeah, no thank you."

Revi reappeared with a sibling next to them. This Patron was a black arachnid like Revi, but easily taller and with different secondary colors. Their eyes, jaw, torso, and claws were red instead of blue. While they also had fluff protecting their neck, they didn't have any on their wrists or ankles. Instead, it sprouted from the top of their head in three spikes like a mohawk. A red triangle sat on their forehead.

The demon gave Darcy duel finger guns. "Hey."

Their voice had a different tone to it, too... a bit older, but still had energy to it. Darcy guessed that this demon was indeed an adult, albeit on the young side. Darcy gave them an uncertain wave.

"Uh... hi. I'm guessing you're Death?"

"The one and only!" They snapped their claws and red sparkles appeared. "My baby sibling told me everything. Said you passed the test and were interested in a job."

"Yeah, that's right. What kind of jobs do you guys do?"

Death crossed their arms in a casual manner. "Well, it's different for each Patron. Revi and their warlocks work in a supporting role. They test out possible new powers and see whether or not they're safe for a warlock to use. They also keep maintenance on pre-existing powers, making sure there aren't any glitches or problems with any updates."

"That can happen?"

Revi said, "The chances are super low, but it's super-duper important to lower that number down to zero. After all, you don't wanna be climbing up really high and then have your sticky powers stop working." Revi put a fist against their chest in pride. "Me and my warlocks make sure that those glitches never happen!"

"Wow. That's actually really cool. But why make updates at all?"

Death explained, "It's important to keep up with the times. Society evolves and so must we."

Revi added, "And sometimes we just get new ideas for new applications of powers! Like the vibration senses. They used to only work on thread-like objects like ropes and webs, but then one of our warlocks got the idea to have it work on structures, too! That way, warlocks can tell how stable a place is and figure out the best route for navigating it."

"Oh, that's sick! I think I could really contribute as a revival warlock. But if it's alright, I'd like to see what the other two Patrons do first."

"Okie-dokie!"

Death stepped forward. "So, I won't beat around the bush, I deal with death. When a person dies, all their memories and experiences form into a single, condensed shape. You might call it a soul. The soul then appears in a world between worlds. When they're ready to move on to the afterlife, the soul goes to me or one of my warlocks and we send them off."

"Wow..." Darcy then asked, "What's the afterlife like?"

Death shrugged. "I wouldn't know. It's a one-way trip, and it's different for every person. Some souls don't even believe in the afterlife and spend their existence hanging out with us."

"Sounds, uh... cool?"

"It isn't for everyone, but it also isn't the only role we have. Some death warlocks work as therapists, for example. Others break up fights between souls. Some help the creatures that live in that world, although I can't explain those without showing you in person."

"I see. That could be interesting. So what about the Life Patron? What do they do?"

"Oh!" Oliver said excitedly. "I can explain that! Life warlocks do stuff that saves lives! It can be direct stuff like helping out in a crisis, but it can also involve little things like delivering medicine or helping someone get food or water."

Death nodded along. "A lot of life warlocks work undercover as superheroes."

"Yeah. I haven't met any other life warlocks, though."

Darcy said, "Yeah, I don't think I've seen any other spider-themed heroes, either. Not lately."

Death said, "I'm not at all surprised—Life Patron is *very* secretive."

Revi said, "Yeah, but they used to be friendly. They've only been like this for a century. That's really not that long."

"Still."

Darcy hummed in thought. "Is there a way for me to talk to Life Patron as well?"

"Sure," Death answered, "But you'd have to meet up with them at a separate location. Life doesn't 'visit' the new hires anymore. I'll write down the address for you."

"Thanks. Oh, and another question: What would happen if I never got hired? What happens if someone turns you guys down?"

"Well, our meeting would seem like a dream and fade away with time, like a sand castle that gets washed away with the tide. 'Course, you being an arachnomorph complicates things, but I guess you would chalk up your transformation as being a mutation or something."

"Ah, that's true. Oh! And one more question!"

"Yes?"

"Revi, do you have the power to resurrect people? I figure 'cuz of your name..."

Revi frowned. "I'm sorry, but that isn't one of my powers. I was born when a mortal had the idea of revival, but I don't think actually doing it is possible."

"Oh."

"I'm sorry. As much as we wanna think we can break that rule, it's as fundamental as gravity." They gave Death a look, "Right, Death?"

Death stared at the floor. "...Right."

Oliver asked, "Are you okay?"

Death immediately smiled. "Yup! Well, we'll leave you to it. I'll let Life know that you wanna talk with them."

"Thanks," Darcy replied. "I appreciate all the help."

With that, both Revi and Death disappeared. Darcy turned to Oliver.

"So you work for Life Patron?"

"Uh-huh. They're not the most, um... emotionally-available, but they care about their warlocks. Um, when I offered to help you get a job, I actually tried calling Life Patron. I guess something happened, though, because they never answered."

"You think something happened to them?"

"I don't know." He rubbed his arm. "They're usually so prompt. I'm kind of worried."

"Well, why don't we leave right now? We'll go to the address Death gave me and check it out. And then... we'll take things from there."

Oliver exhaled. "Yeah."

Life Patron

Dawn transitioned into morning and the sky became soft green. Darcy couldn't remember the last time they had a reason to wear day clothes. It was nice to dress in something that wasn't a work uniform for once. The problem came when they had to put on the clothes, however.

Darcy's jacket was made for humans, obviously, with only two sleeves to fit arms into. Darcy had to fold their extra arms around their torso, then zip up the jacket. It wasn't too noticeable as long as they didn't undo the zipper or try to move the extra limbs. Unfortunately, Darcy just couldn't figure out a way to fit into their pants.

How do Venutians fit their abdomens into things? I'll have to find a Venus-style clothing store when I have some money. And if anyone asks, I'll tell them that I'm a white bumble bee and my jacket's hiding my wings. As long as I act like I belong, I should be fine. Haha, "bee" fine.

Darcy ultimately accepted the loss and went without pants—it wasn't like anything was showing, after all. With their drawstring bag in tow, they followed Oliver out and down the fire escape.

"If I may ask," Said Oliver, "How did you choose the name Darcy?"

"I found it in a book. To be honest, I just liked the sound of it."

"I was named Oliver because of my eyes. Apparently, I also had a name tag that read 'Vermilio', so that's how I got my last name. Orphanage never saw who dropped me off, though..."

"Well, I think Oliver is a lovely name."

"Thanks, you too."

As they made their way to the destination, Darcy heard Oliver whispering something. They leaned in close to listen.

"DarcyDarcyDarcyDarcy.   Their   name   is   Darcy. DarcyDarcyDarcyDarcy..."

Their heart had never felt so warm.

Oliver then asked aloud, "So if you choose an employer, will you become a superhero?"

"Not gonna lie, it's super-tempting, pardon the pun. I don't know if I'd make a good hero, though."

"If you want, I can teach you what I know. I have years of training in combat."

"I appreciate the offer, but I was thinking about other stuff. Like, a common thing for superheroes is that they have a secret identity, right?"

"Unless they're registered, yeah. But you can have a public identity even if you aren't registered."

"Yeah, but that wouldn't be very smart 'cuz then any enemies I make could just target my loved ones."

"Oh, true. I guess that's the burden of being a hero... you can't tell your loved ones the truth about yourself."

"Well, I don't know about *that* part."

"Pardon?"

"Why *not* tell your friends and family about your hero life? Not as a public thing, but as extra security."

"I'm afraid I don't understand."

"Okay, so a trope for superheroes is when their personal life and hero life collide. The hero has to leave to do hero things and the loved ones are like, 'Where did they go? Why did they run off?' and then get angry at them for abandoning them in a dangerous situation. And then the hero is all, 'Woe is me, there is no way to fix this.' But like... dude. Just tell them. If you can't deal with the drama of a double life, then involve the people you trust. And you know what? Becoming a hero kinda puts them in danger anyways."

Oliver tilted his head to the side. "How so?"

"Say that you don't tell your loved ones about your hero life. Then one day, you're fighting a villain and they figure out your identity. They're gonna target the loved ones to make you hurt, right? And since they've been kept in the dark, they'll be completely unprepared. But if you *do* tell them about the possible risks of being connected to you, then you can work together to make tactics and backup plans. *And* it lets them consent on whether or not they want to be in that kind of relationship. Like, seriously, not telling people the dangers they could be put in is like moving into a house without installing a fire alarm."

Oliver put a hand to his chin. "Hm... I guess I never looked at it that way before. I suppose a superhero *does* have some personal responsibility when it comes to choosing who to stay in contact with. But what if this hypothetical hero decides to cut off contact with their loved ones? Then they technically wouldn't be in danger anymore."

"True, yeah. I guess isolation *would* keep the people around you safe... 'cuz you wouldn't have anyone around you at all."

"Maybe that's why superhero teams exist... not just to handle large threats, but for the sense of community that they bring. They could have people to form bonds with without that extra fear."

"Oh, true. So what do you do, Oliver? How do *you* protect your family?"

Oliver looked away. "I, uh... Mister Harrell is kind of my family. He's like a father to me, you know? But other than him... I just have you."

"You don't team up with other heroes? Not even for crossover events?"

"I'm not really... *allowed* to be with the other heroes." Oliver cleared his throat. "But you know, it's alright. I'll live."

Oliver fiddled with his mask to ensure that it was still turned off. Darcy thought over his statement.

Why would Harrell not want Oliver around other superheroes?

It was another thing they had to drop for now, as the duo arrived at their destination.

The address belonged to an abandoned building in the quiet part of town. It used to be a multi-story art studio, but it was damaged in a battle between a hero and a villain. Neither of the superpeople were registered and the building wasn't insured, so the owner couldn't afford to repair the damages. Thus, the building was condemned. Although most of the windows and doors had been boarded up, a gaping hole had been left open with nothing but a single warning sign next to it.

Oliver placed a hand against a wall. He knocked against it with his other hand. After a few moments, he said,

"Most of the building is still sound. We'll be fine as long as we don't use super strength on anything."

Darcy stared at him, fascinated. "Woah. You can tell all that just by touching it?"

"It's one of the spider powers. I can analyze objects just by focusing on their vibrations."

"That is *so* cool."

Oliver stepped back and rubbed his arm. "Ah. Well. You know. I, uh..."

"Lemme try!"

Darcy mimicked Oliver's technique. While they sensed vibrations, they had no idea what they meant.

"Get anything?" Oliver asked.

"Not really." They sighed. "It's like listening to a language I don't understand."

Oliver put a hand on their shoulder. "Well, when you- I mean *if* you- become a warlock, I can teach you what I know."

"Thanks, man."

Darcy gingerly stepped into the building. They followed Oliver's lead, making sure not to stray too far from him.

A voice echoed from an upper floor, "Up here. The stairs are stable."

Darcy didn't answer out of fear.

"I know you are there," Said the voice. "I can feel your presence. Both of you."

Oliver sighed with relief. "That's Life's voice."

Darcy sighed as well. "Oh, thank god."

The duo followed the voice. It sounded as old as Death's, but with an even tone. While Death spoke like a chill friend, Life spoke like a stern professional. Darcy and Oliver inched up the stairs and peeked into the second floor. A wooden desk and chairs stood in the middle of the floor. A demon sat patiently with their claws intertwined together.

They looked just like Death, perhaps just an inch or so taller. Their eyes, jaw, torso, and claws were all green. They didn't have any extra fluff on their body, but the fluff around their neck seemed extra dense. They had a green V-shaped symbol on their forehead.

Life's eyes widened. "Red Arachnid!"

"Hi, Life!" He gave them a wave. "I'm so glad you're alright. How have you been?"

"Surprised. I'm glad to see you safe, though. I can't remember the last time one of my-"

Life stopped and stared at Darcy. They looked at their paper notes.

"Ah. You must be Revi's... patient."

Darcy shrugged. "I guess so."

"My siblings told me everything. Are you certain you're alright with being an arachnomorph?"

"I mean, is there a way to change back?"

"No."

"Then why ask?"

"Because I want to know something. Revi offered to transform you because your future looked bleak. It was even possible that your life was on the line."

"Yeah?"

"Then I must ask... if the situation weren't so dire and there were no consequences to staying human, then would you have still chosen to transform? Would you still have become what you are now?"

Darcy considered this. "Honestly? I think so."

"But what about your humanity?"

"What about it? I mean... what's so special about being human, anyway? It can't be sapience—Venutians have that, too. Can't be empathy—there are plenty of humans who have low empathy. So what's left? Cooking? Pretty sure I can still cook as a spider."

"So you don't view humanity as something special? Something that places you above other species?"

"I certainly hope not. I mean, if anything, I think I'm appreciating being a spider already."

"Oh?"

"Yeah, like having an exoskeleton instead of skin. No dryness, no peeling, no acne, no cutting myself on bread..."

Oliver asked, "Darcy, how in the world do you cut yourself on bread?"

"It was really sharp bread! It was well-toasted and the crust was stiff. I tried to break it into smaller pieces, but the bread was so tough and broke in a weird way, so the crust had jagged edges. I got a scar from it!" They showed Oliver their left hand, only to realize that it had no scars. "Er, well, I don't anymore, but still."

"Hm. Well, true." Oliver then added with a lighthearted tone, "And spiders don't have bones, so you won't have to worry about breaking them."

"Yeah! And no spine means no back problems. That'll be nice."

"Oh, that sounds *really* nice." Oliver pressed his hands against his back and stretched. "Being tall means that your back *hates* you, ugh. And don't get me started on the knees."

"And I have extra arms now! I'll be able to carry so many groceries with these! Multitasking just got so much easier."

Life put a palm forward. "I see your point. However, there are other things to discuss. Please sit down."

Darcy sat opposite of Life. Oliver stood by Darcy's side. He said,

"Life Patron, before we begin, I just want you to know that Darcy is a hard worker with a strong spirit. They care about other people and are highly intelligent. They would make a strong addition to us, not just as a warlock, but also as a friend."

The way he spoke about them made Darcy's heart swell. There was something comforting about knowing that he felt the same way about them as they did about him.

Life hummed in thought. "Yes, from what I have heard, this person does seem to prove their intelligence. At the very least, they were smart enough to learn more before making a decision. I respect that."

*I wouldn't call myself **that** smart. Probably shouldn't say that out loud, though...*

Darcy said, "It, uh, just seems like common sense."

"We could always use more of that." Life looked at their notes. "Red Arachnid, I must ask you to leave the room for the rest of this conversation."

Oliver nodded. He backed away, but not before giving Darcy a dual thumbs-up. He whispered,

"I believe in you!"

Once he had left the room, Life looked Darcy dead in the eyes. They observed Darcy with a sort of glare that one may find on a hawk. Life spoke slowly and sternly.

"We try to keep our existence a secret in this world. If the wrong people found out, they would siphon our power and use it for their own selfish ends. Currently, your existence could lead them to us. Draw the wrong attention, or say the wrong thing to the wrong person..."

Darcy gulped. "I promise not to expose you guys to the public. If I were in your shoes, I wouldn't want to have my existence revealed without my consent either."

"Then you understand how careful we must be." Life's stare pierced Darcy's soul. They said in a low voice,

"What is to keep us from hiding you in a pocket dimension in isolation for the rest of your life?"

Darcy shrank into their seat. They fought the waver in their voice.

"I-I believe that... that doing that would be against what you three represent. From what I understand, you each represent life, death, and revival. But... what life could I have if I'm trapped in a pocket dimension? It would be an empty one. And what kind of death would that then be? Can it even be considered a death if it's just withering away into oblivion? And Revi already told me that they can't resurrect people. There would be no revival in that existence; just eternal rot. Doing this, it would be against... everything."

Life observed Darcy in silence. Darcy held tightly onto their chair. Their extra arms squirmed in the confines of their jacket. If they still had skin, it would be sweating right now. They didn't dare blink.

Life nodded and looked back to their papers. "You passed the test."

Darcy let out a heavy breath. They let go of the chair, only to realize that their claws had left indents into it.

"Ah... sorry."

"It is no issue. Chairs are replaceable."

"But, uh... what *would* happen if I didn't become an employee? Death said that my memory of you would fade, but how would I make a living?"

"The last time we transformed someone into an arachnomorph, it was in 1915. The patient in question elected to simply live in the countryside until he passed from old age. According to Death, he had quite the lucrative fishing career. In this day and age, however, I am not certain if that level of peace is possible."

"Yeah, but with all the different ways for people to get superpowers, I could just make up random bullshit. Hell, there's a member of the West Coasters who got his powers from a lightning strike. Just a simple lightning strike! Shit's wild."

"But that is no reason not to be careful. Do not stray into malicious hands. Do not make a fool of yourself."

"I know. I wasn't born yesterday."

"You may have been born twenty-five years ago, but that is hardly a blink for a creature such as I. There is so little of the world that you know."

"I'm well aware. That's why I'm interested in this job."

"And if you chose to work with us, who would you pick? This will not affect the results of the interview."

"Hm... if I can ask, what would be *your* personal preference?"

"Mine?" Life thought for a moment. "I suppose I would suggest working with Death or Revi. With Death, you could easily build a life within the realm of the dead. It is invisible to the living, so you would be the safest there. As for Revi, they do actually have pocket dimensions, but those ones are populated with their employees and full of life. There is never a dull day with Revi. If it were up to me, I would do what would allow me to live the longest."

Makes sense that the representation of Life would say that.

"Now, shall we begin the interview proper?"

Darcy sat up straight. "Right. Yeah."

"You *do* have what it takes to work for me, if that is what you wish. Just as with Death and Revi, you would receive pizzazz."

"Pizzazz?"

"The power that flows through us." Life looked back to their papers. "Have Death or Revi explained it to you yet?"

"From context clues, I think I understand it? Warlocks get their powers from pieces of Patrons, and that power is called pizzazz. So warlocks also have pizzazz?"

"That is correct. For creatures like Patrons, pizzazz makes up our very existence. For organic creatures, it simply adds onto existing organs."

"Like a symbiosis?"

"In a way. It's similar to electricity, so it binds itself to the nervous system. It connects to the electrical signals given off by the brain and allows the user to consciously use the power it gives."

Darcy scratched their head. "Sorry, I don't know a lot about science. What do you mean exactly?"

"Warlocks activate their powers via thought. Think about using super strength and it activates. Focus on sticking to a surface and you will stick. And like anything connected to the nervous system, the more experienced you become, the more naturally you will use the power. Of course, given your unique situation, you already have powers."

"Yeah, what does that mean for me?"

"Well, you currently have all the basic spider powers- strength, agility, stickiness, and vibration senses- but if you became a warlock, you would also be able to gain extra powers. Revi and their warlocks are constantly working to perfect and come up with new abilities to use."

"Oh yeah. Not to mention the free food."

"Yes, many people become warlocks for that reason. But we are getting off-track here. I must warn you about something when it comes to pizzazz: in attaching itself to your mind, it also attaches itself to your memories. After getting pizzazz, it will be bonded to every new memory you create. This means that if you were to ever lose that pizzazz, you would also lose all of those memories."

"What? Even stuff that isn't warlock-related?"

"Yes. You would still recall everything leading up to becoming a warlock, but afterwards..."

"All blank." Darcy ran a hand through their head-fuzz. "God.... So this would be all or nothing, huh? I can't just work for a few years and then quit."

Life nodded. "Precisely. Quitting or getting fired would result in the removal of your pizzazz."

"Okay. I see." Darcy exhaled. "I have another question."

"Yes?"

"Am I allowed to work with other employees? Like, if two life employees work together to save someone, what happens? Who gets the reward?"

"Both of them. We support cooperation."

"Cool. And what are the rules? What would cause a job termination?"

"Generally speaking, there are two actions that would result in termination: the first is revealing the existence of Patrons, pizzazz, and/

or warlocks. The second is killing another employee, no matter what the justification."

"Really? But what if an employee's a horrible person or a murderer? Or just... really annoying?"

"Then they are to be taken to Patron Court. If the case against them is strong enough, we will fire them. Violence between employees is strictly off-limits."

"I see, okay."

"Are you *planning* on attacking anyone?"

"No, no! Just... wanted to know where the line was drawn."

"Hm." Life conjured a manila folder in a flurry of green sparkles. "There are also rules specific to each theme. Revival: do not lie about, nor tamper with, test results. Death: do not prevent a soul from passing to the afterlife unless they explicitly request it, and do not intentionally harm an otherbeing. Life: do not intentionally endanger or take a life."

"What about killing in self-defense, or if you need to doom one person to save the other?"

"Those are handled on a case-by-case basis. Do you have any further questions?"

"Hm... do you have a full list of unlockable powers? Your siblings mentioned them, but nothing exhaustive."

Life pulled out a sheet of lined paper. "Keep in mind that these are only the current available powers. They are subject to be updated or changed to best suit the needs of the employees."

Darcy scanned the list.

Claws, Barbs, Venom Glands, Form Change...

"Huh. What is Form Change?"

"Ah. That one is terribly unpopular. It would allow the user to shift into a more arachnid-like form. You could choose between the spider form, which is agile, or the tarantula form, which is powerful. There are a number of customization options as well, such as choosing the colors and amount of setae."

"I guess that one would be redundant for me, huh?"

"Not necessarily. These particular designs for the spider and tarantula forms are specially crafted to have mass appeal among general audiences. If you want an appearance that is less... alien... you may want to consider unlocking the Form Change ability. That is, if you do choose to work with us."

"Hm..."

"We are actually considering removing that ability from the active list. After all, most of our employees these days are humans. In the past twenty years, only two employees have picked up Form Change. It is simply not viable in this day and age."

"But even if *all* the employees were human, there's still a chance that someone might want to use it."

Life grimaced. "*Why*? Humans find us disgusting and horrible. They call us monsters and trap us in cages. Not even spider-based superheroes are loved; many of my employees had quit for one reason or another. They don't even talk to me anymore." They hissed, "They probably think my siblings and I are freaks."

"Hey, don't say that. Maybe they're just really busy, or just needed a break." Something then occurred to Darcy. "Or maybe there's a break in connection. After all, Red Arachnid hasn't been able to contact you, yet he's clearly still working for you."

"Excuse me?"

"He said he tried to call you earlier today."

"Really? I received nothing. Yet, when he was in the room, I still sensed his life energy." Life considered this. "Maybe... could it be something on my end? I will have to look into this."

"Is there a way to manually check in on your employees?"

Life shook their head. "I can only appear in places where there are no civilian witnesses, and in the world of heroes and villains, someone is always watching. Even if I knew where they were, I couldn't visit them if I tried."

"I see..." *If I become a superhero, I'll have to be careful.*

Life said, "But we had gotten off-track. Are there any final questions you would like to ask?"

"No, I believe that was my last question. I think I want to work for you guys, but I'd like to think it over before I decide which one."

"Very well. Here is the contract." Life conjured a multi-page manuscript. "This contract reiterates everything we discussed as well as anything else you may need to know. When you are ready, sign it with the name you wish us to call you by. The three of us will then appear. Give the contract to the one you wish to work for. Keep in mind that to everyone but you, the contents of this contract will appear blank."

"Understood. Thank you." Darcy rolled up the contract and held it under their arm. "Actually, one last question occurred to me."

"Yes?"

"I've noticed that there is a symbol on your forehead. Same for Death and Revi. What do they mean?"

Life curled their claws around their mouth. "Hm. How do I explain this in a way a mortal would understand... ah." They held a palm upward and a small hologram appeared in their hand. It showed four spider beings.

"The first Patron had one line. The second Patron- me- has two lines, which create the V shape that you see. The third Patron- Death- has three lines and the fourth Patron, being Revi, has four. If another Patron was born, they would have five lines."

"Oh, wow. So who was the first Patron?"

"Someone you cannot meet. Now apologies, but I must be going now."

"Uh, okay. Thank you for this opportunity."

Life nodded and disappeared.

Darcy returned downstairs, where Oliver waited. He held his hands together.

"So? How did it go?"

"I think it went pretty well. I told them that I wanted to look over things one more time. I'm gonna head home now so I can go do that."

"Okay. I should, um... get back to the headquarters. Mister Harrell gets angry when he doesn't know where I am." He turned his mask back on. "See you next time!"

Darcy gave him a wave. "Yeah! See ya tomorrow."

Decision

Back home, Darcy entered through the fire escape so they wouldn't have to pass through the lobby. They took off their jacket and set it on a chair. Hiding their extra limbs wasn't uncomfortable, per se, but it was still nice to let their body breathe a bit more. They noticed the comforter that was still balled up in the corner of the room. Its stench had gotten worse since a few hours ago, like a rotting human corpse.

Damn, what am I gonna do with that? Should I just throw it into the dumpster? Is that, like... biologically safe?

A quick internet search informed them that as long as the corpse in question was not eaten or placed near water, it would be alright. So, Darcy (quite awkwardly) carried the comforter down the fire escape and placed it in the dumpster. They glanced around to ensure nobody saw the action, then climbed back into their apartment. They washed their hands for good measure.

Guess I can cross "disposing my own remains" off of the bucket list. Ahahaha... don't think about it. Back to business.

Darcy set the contract onto the kitchen table and analyzed it line by line. Most of its contents had already been discussed with the three Patrons, but Darcy wanted to ensure that they didn't miss anything. This paid off, as there was a page focused exclusively on being an arachnomorph. It read,

"This is Life. I wrote this page to help you adjust to your new body. While you seemed at ease with your condition, there may be certain aspects that you are not aware of, and I felt it necessary for you to know these details."

Darcy flipped open their brick of a phone. With the press of a button, a tactile keyboard unfolded from the bottom half of the phone. Despite working for Almond Industries, Darcy always preferred the Vance-brand technology, specifically for its bulkiness and longevity. They typed down the following information in case they ever forgot it.

"Externally, arachnomorphs resemble spiders with an anthropomorphic body type. Internally, they are a mix of species with some artistic liberties from my siblings and I.

"The teeth are sharp enough to cut most materials and strong enough to handle metal, but if you find yourself with a broken or missing tooth, eat foods with high mineral counts, such as cheese, nuts, and fish. Your body will restore dental damage in a couple weeks' time.

"Your heart and lungs are still in the same location as they were before your transformation and work similarly to a human's. This gives you greater aerobic abilities than a typical spider, but try not to push yourself too hard.

"You may have noticed that your digestive system continues into your opisthosoma, otherwise known as the abdomen. The exit for your digestive system is in the central posterior point of the opisthosoma while the exit for your silk is in the distal posterior section. Please do not get them confused."

Darcy thought to themself, *I'm starting to think this was written for someone smarter than me.*

They continued reading.

"Because your major organs are not in the opisthosoma, the body part in question has much more room for other biological mechanics, specifically silk glands. Because of this, you can create many types of silk. And while your size proportionately grants you more silk than mundane spiders, it is not infinite. To ensure that you do not run out, it is recommended that you eat foods high in fiber and protein, such as meats and oats.

"One curiosity- or concern- you may have is whether or not arachnomorphs can reproduce. They cannot. They lack any and all reproductive organs and do not produce the associated hormones. Although arachnomorphs are exceedingly rare in this day and age, if one were to reproduce, the resulting spiderlings would draw too much attention. Our apologies if giving birth was a goal in your life."

Tch. Like hell it was. Okay, one last paragraph...

"Mundane spiders only molt until they reach maturity, but the process of molting is incredibly useful for healing wounds. A new exoskeleton is grown, complete with renewed limbs and setae. It is like a second birth. For this reason, my siblings and I have set arachnomorphs to molt once a year, in the springtime. The season represents rebirth, after all.

"And with that, we thank you for your time. Please take care of yourself. If you choose not to work with us, then we hope that the life you have is a safe and happy one."

Revi had mentioned a molt in the spring. I'll definitely want to write that one down. It also sounds like these guys have some level of control over what arachnomorph bodies can do. Are they like software updates, where the changes are universal, or are they like phones, where only the latest ones get the new stuff? If the Patrons make a change to how arachnomorphs work, will I get a say in it?

Darcy's thoughts wandered as they typed down miscellaneous notes.

Should I give myself a secret identity? I want to live my life as Darcy, but having an alias while working would be the smart thing to do. Then again, the only people who know that Darcy even exists are Oliver and my mom.

Besides, how would I even keep a secret identity with a body like this? I'd have to wear a full-body costume like Oliver. But that looks so tight and uncomfortable... no idea how he does any jumps or flips in that. I suppose I could choose a name for the symbolism.

Darcy then made a list of possible superhero names.

Maybe my favorite flower, Dandelion. No, too docile... no villain would fear someone named Dandelion. How about my favorite animal? Nah, that wouldn't work, it would clash with the spider theme. Although... I guess I could confuse my enemies with a name like that. If I name myself Rabbit Hero, then people would assume I would have rabbit weaknesses, not spider *weaknesses. Wait, what **are** rabbits weak to? Foxes? Victor Quartermaine? Pesticides? Then again, spiders are probably weak to pesticides, too...*

They looked outside. They still longed for the weather from back home. Sure, California was great, but even after living here for years, Darcy was uncertain if they would ever prefer this place.

They went to their bedroom and looked at a family photo. Darcy, their mother, and their father all ate a banana split together at their favorite family restaurant. Darcy would never forget that day. With a bittersweet smile, they typed onto their phone,

Banana Split.

Their phone then buzzed with an alert: their mother had just sent a text letting them know how she was and asking how they were. It was just a standard, casual message, but Darcy looked down at themself and hesitated. They mentally ran through some possible greetings.

"Hey, mom. So, uh, I'm a spider now."

"Hey mom! Guess who lost their humanity? Don't worry, I'm fine."

"So, mom, I may have experienced a permanent transformation."

"Good news, mom: Julia doesn't exist anymore. Bad news: I might... scare you."

Darcy paced through the kitchen with the phone in their claws.

No, no. Mom wouldn't be afraid of me. She worked with a bunch of Venutians. They are arthropods and I'm an arthropod... it'll be fine. Everything will be fine.

Still, before Darcy could call their mother, they would first have to pick a lie. They couldn't tell their mother about the Patrons, not even with a hint; Darcy didn't want to do anything that could risk them losing this opportunity.

*God damn it, now **I'm** one of those heroes who doesn't tell their family shit. That's what I get for tempting fate.*

They cycled through possible cover stories.

"I volunteered for a science experiment."

"I had a bad allergic reaction to a spider bite."

"I got cursed by the Macbeths." No, she'd never believe that...

Darcy stopped pacing. Could they really lie to their own mother? Ever since the relocation, she had been the only person Darcy could be a hundred percent honest to. Now they had to make something up to keep a secret that they only just learned about.

Isolation can keep civilian lives safe...

Darcy sat back down with a sigh. They sent a simple text that said they were doing okay.

Sorry, mom.

They spent the rest of their time rereading the contract, checking for anything they may have missed. Questions lingered at the back of their mind: what would their new life be like? What kind of dangers would they run into? What kind of allies and enemies would they make?

Part of them was tempted to simply choose Life so they could work with Red Arachnid, but Darcy also knew that it could be unwise to pick a career just to be with someone. After all, Oliver had his own life to live; Darcy didn't want to weigh him down with any issues they would bring to the table. Plus, there was always the chance that the two could ultimately become incompatible as friends. Something could always drive them apart, and then where would Darcy be?

Just like my last friendship...

Darcy gave a weary sigh. It may be paranoia, but they still readied themself for any loneliness they may feel in the future, as well as any troubles they may encounter.

Well, whichever employer I choose... I know I'm gonna have a heck of an adventure.

— — —

Late morning brought with it the golden light of the sun. Darcy watched the kitchen window in anticipation of both the coming day and their visitors. Their breath held in anticipation, they signed the contract.

Darcy Aran.

The three appeared. Standing next to the others made it apparent that Revi was half a foot shorter than their siblings. They held their hands behind their back and wore a polite smile. Death, meanwhile, leaned slightly with a hand on their hip. They gave Darcy a wave, to which Darcy waved back. Life stood as straight as a plank with their arms at their sides.

Darcy's heartbeat quickened. They were nearly too afraid to stand up. It wasn't just the Patrons' appearances that unnerved them, although that was also true, but they carried a certain presence as well. Revi's blue, Death's red, Life's green—their colors seemed to emanate energy. Or perhaps it was power Darcy felt, or perhaps knowledge, or perhaps a representation of the unknown itself. Darcy's heart beat even faster. They felt like a skydiver about to jump.

"Are you okay?" Revi asked. "Should we come later?"

"No, no. Sorry. I'm just... wow. This is happening. I'm becoming a warlock. This is so cool!"

"Heck yeah we are," Death cheered. "I'm so hyped!"

Life asked, "Have you decided which to work with yet?"

"Yeah, actually. I've thought it over and made my decision. While all three of you seem really cool, I think there is one I would like to work with the most. I think I will go with..."

Don't miss out!

Visit the website below and you can sign up to receive emails whenever Sol Quasar publishes a new book. There's no charge and no obligation.

https://books2read.com/r/B-A-MBMIC-OOQDF

BOOKS 2 READ

Connecting independent readers to independent writers.

Also by Sol Quasar

Banana Split Timeline
BST Book Zero
Death Timeline
Life Timeline
Revival Timeline

About the Author

Sol Quasar chose their name to represent outer space, something that they have always loved. The wonder of the stars remains constant in their life. Along with writing books, Sol enjoys petting cats, taking photos of spiders, and drawing art. They hope that their stories can help other people someday.

Sol currently lives in Wisconsin, but prefers to keep specific information obscured.